A MERIT BADGE MYSTERY

D0832222

The Berenstain BEAR SCOUTS
AND THE
MISSING MERIT BADGES

ISBN 0-590-56390-4

Copyright © 1998 by Berenstain Enterprises, Inc.
All rights reserved. Published by Scholastic Inc.
SCHOLASTIC, CARTWHEEL BOOKS and the CARTWHEEL BOOKS logo
are trademarks and/or registered trademarks of Scholastic Inc.
Merit Badge Mystery is a trademark of Berenstain Enterprises.

Library of Congress Cataloging-in-Publication Data available

LC: 97-50466

10 9 8 7 6 5 4 3 2   8 9/9 0/0 01 02

Printed in the U.S.A.
First printing, September 1998

The Berenstain BEAR SCOUTS AND THE MISSING MERIT BADGES

A MERIT BADGE MYSTERY

Stan & Jan Berenstain

Illustrated by Michael Berenstain

Cartwheel
·B·O·O·K·S·®
SCHOLASTIC INC.
New York Toronto London Auckland Sydney

"They're gone! All gone!" cried Scout Sister. She was the first one into the Scouts' clubhouse. The Scouts had made their clubhouse from an old chicken coop. It did not have a door. The only way in was through a hollow tree.

"What's all gone?" asked Scout Brother. He was the second one into the clubhouse.

"Our merit badges!" cried Scout Sister. "Our beautiful merit badges! We worked so hard to earn them!"

Scout Fred and Scout Lizzy were also
upset. The Bear Scouts were very proud of
their merit badges. Not only had the Scouts
worked hard to earn them, the badges were
very colorful and very beautiful.

There was the Good Deed badge. It showed the Bear Scouts helping an older bear across the street.

There was the Nature Lovers Badge. It showed the Bear Scouts hugging a tree.

There was the Starfinders Badge. This one showed the Bear Scouts looking up at the Big Dipper. There were many other badges, too.

The Bear Scouts were sad.

The Bear Scouts were upset.

The Bear Scouts were *furious*!

Their precious merit badges were gone, missing, stolen away! Who could have taken them?

It was a mystery — the mystery of the missing merit badges!

"We must solve the mystery!" said Scout Brother. "First we must look for clues!"

Scout Sister slipped on some garbage. "Oops!" she said. "Which careless person left this garbage lying about?"

"That's not garbage," said Scout Fred.
"That's a clue."

"Hmm," said Scout Brother,
"a banana peel, some pea pods, and some
corn cobs."

"I hear a snuffling, chomping sound,"
said Scout Lizzy.

The sound came from Mrs. Pig's pen. She was eating her favorite food—garbage.

"Mrs. Pig," said Brother. "Someone has stolen our merit badges. Do you know who?"

Mrs. Pig chomped away at her lunch. "I haven't a clue," she said.

"Maybe not," said Scout Sister. "But *we do*! And here it is!"

"A banana peel, pea pods, and corn cobs," said Mrs. Pig. "Sorry, not my kind of garbage. As you can see, I prefer apple cores, potato peelings, and broccoli stalks. Besides, I'm too big to fit through the hole in your hollow tree. But I have a mystery for you. Somebody stole my gold nose ring while I was asleep. If it turns up, will you please let me know?"

"Hmm,"
said Lizzy.
"Who's black
and white and
answers to the
name 'Bossie'?"
"Mrs. Cow!"
cried Sister.

"Mrs. Cow," said Brother.
"Someone has stolen our merit badges.
Do you know who?"

Mrs. Cow munched on some
dandelions. "I haven't a clue,"
she said.

"Maybe not," said Sister. "But *we do*! And here it is!"

"That fur is not mine," said Mrs. Cow. "My fur is short and smooth. Besides, I'm much too big to fit through the hole in your hollow tree. But I have a mystery for you. Someone stole my calf's silver bell. If it turns up, would you please let me know?"

"Sure," said Brother. "But what
we need now is another clue."
"Look!" said Fred. "A tin can lid!"

"Hmm," said Lizzy, "who eats tin cans and likes to butt Farmer Ben with his horns?"
"Mr. Goat!" cried Sister.

"Mr. Goat," said Brother. "Someone has stolen our merit badges. Do you know who?"

Mr. Goat sharpened his horns on a rock. "I haven't a clue," he said.

"Maybe not," said Sister. "But *we do*! And here it is!"

"I'm off tin cans. They upset my stomach," said Mr. Goat. "I'm on a soft diet now. Besides, my horns are much too big to fit through the hole in your hollow tree. But I have a mystery for you. Someone has stolen my prize blue ribbon that I won at the fair. If it turns up, would you please let me know?"

The Bear Scouts nodded yes, but they were discouraged. "What should we do?" said Sister.

"We're fresh out of clues," said Fred.

"And there's no one left to ask," said Lizzy.

"Oh, but there is!" said Brother.
"We can ask Dr. Wise Old Owl."

"Of course!" said Sister.
"Dr. Wise Old Owl knows everything."

"Dr. Wise Old Owl! Dr. Wise Old
Owl!" called Brother. "Someone has
stolen our merit badges. Do you know
who?"

Dr. Wise Old Owl poked his head out of his hole in the hollow tree. "Whooo!" said Dr. Wise Old Owl.

Who took your badges?
Well, you may ask —
It was no robber,
Though he wore a robber's mask.

Then he yawned a big yawn and went back into his hole.

"It was no robber?" said Scout Sister.

"Even though he wore a robber's mask?" said Scout Fred.

"Who can it be?" asked Lizzy.

As the Bear Scouts sat and thought, the sun began to set. "Look!" cried Lizzy. The Scouts saw Mr. Raccoon coming out of his den for his nightly prowl.

The Bear Scouts knew three things about Mr. Raccoon. He was fond of garbage, loved brightly colored and shiny things, and *wore a robber's mask!*

When Mr. Raccoon was out of sight, Sister, who was the smallest Scout, crawled into his den and found the missing merit badges — along with Mrs. Pig's gold nose ring, Mrs. Cow's calf's silver bell, Mr. Goat's prize blue ribbon, and the tin can.

After putting the tin can in the recycling bin, the Scouts returned the missing things to their rightful owners.

They put their hard-earned merit badges back in their rightful clubhouse place. They also made a door for their hollow tree so there wouldn't be a next time. After all, Mr. Raccoon couldn't help himself.

Their only regret was that they couldn't earn a new merit badge for their trouble. They looked in the merit badge book but there was no Missing Merit Badge Merit Badge!